D1003060

MODERN
MASSACRES

MODERN MASSACRES

Short Stories by Timothy Willis Sanders

ISBN 978-1-945028-43-4

First published by Publishing Genius Press
in June 2022, Atlanta, Georgia

Cover art by Christa Palazzolo
Book design by Adam Robinson

Earlier versions of these stories were published in *The Nervous Breakdown,*
Western Beefs of North America, and *LIT Magazine*

Twitter: @timothysanders | @pubgen
www.publishinggenius.com

MODERN
MASSACRES

TIMOTHY WILLIS SANDERS

PUBLISHING
GENIUS PRESS

CONTENTS

ARIZONA

I heard dad say, "Arizona is too hot. He'll burn up."

Would I actually burn up?

Mom knelt down in front of me and took me by the shoulders. She said dad broke a promise. She asked if I would live with her and Uncle Taylor in Arizona. I didn't know what to say. Uncle Taylor was a war hero who had a gold-plated TV-phone, she added, trying to entice me. Before I answered, I wanted to know what dad had to say. He didn't say anything, except that Arizona is too hot, and that I'd burn up.

We raced our Big Wheels six times. Each time, Tony beat us by a stretch. The Malinowski twins, Cal and Carl, were pleading for a seventh race when Tamika ran up to us.

"Look-it what I found! Look-it. Look-it," she said, pointing to the large palm tree a couple houses down.

"Shut up Tamika," Cal said.

Tony guided his Big Wheel to the curb and began following Tamika to the tree. Without thinking, I did the same. Cal and Carl groaned, but left their Big Wheels in the middle of the street and followed us.

"Terry, baby! Time to call your father!" mom yelled from the porch.

Before we moved to Arizona, I asked mom to tell me more about Uncle Taylor's TV-phone.

"The TV is bigger than the couch," she said, "You put in people's number's on the remote control. You can hear the other person's voice through hidden speakers in the living room."

The TV-phone was the first thing I looked for when we arrived at Uncle Taylor's house. What I found was a normal-sized TV, encased in a wooden hutch, not gold, but it did make calls.

My last call with dad, on the normal kitchen phone, was awkward. I couldn't understand him. I held up the phone and shrugged at mom. She took the phone, heard dad's slurred voice, and hung up. She disappeared and I didn't see her for the rest of the night.

This time around we'd use the TV-phone, so Uncle Taylor and mom could hear if dad slurred.

I sat on the couch, legs hanging over the edge, and listened to the ring fill the living room. Between rings, a buzzing teased the middle of my brain. I thought of the palm tree. What did Tamika find? What are Tony and the boys doing about it? The buzzing stopped and a gentle whooshing came through the speakers.

"Dad?" I said, cocking my head. I hoped he had dropped the line.

I heard his voice: "Hell-o SN. HRUB-Doin...."

"Uh, I'm okay," I said, unsure if I was okay, or if he'd asked if I was okay. Or asked a question at all.

Mom jumped off the couch and said, "This is the last time!" She grabbed the remote from Uncle Taylor and hung up on dad. She threw the remote on the couch, put her hands on her hips and stared through the wall. I didn't know what to do.

"Can I go back outside now?"

"Yes. Go," said Uncle Taylor.

He stood and hugged mom.

I ran outside.

In Indiana, I could take a piece of bark off a tree and throw it like a ninja star. From a low branch, I could hoist myself up the tree for a sweeping view of the neighborhood. On Uncle Taylor's block in Phoenix, there was one palm tree that felt largely useless to me. It was too high to climb and provided almost no shade. Tufts of stringy bark stuffed between huge wooden scales covered the tree's trunk. You couldn't make ninja-anything out of the stringy bark, but Tony showed us you could gather some of it under a magnifying glass and it would turn to ash without ever catching fire. That was the only other time we thought of the tree until today.

I walked over to my friends, all of them staring up the palm tree trunk. I saw a black growth at the base of a branch. As I got closer, I realized it was a beehive, and I sprinted towards the tree.

Uncle Taylor met us at the airport. He gave mom a long hug and called me "young man." He took our luggage and we followed him to his Jeep. I watched him take the top cover off the Jeep, fold it neatly, and place it in the trunk, next to our luggage. He picked me up by my overalls and set me in the backseat, fastening my seatbelt before giving my head a swift, affectionate rub.

As we drove down the highway, the dry air whipped through the Jeep and wrote me out of their conversation. I looked at my uncle. There was a coin-sized speck of sunlight on his bald head. He had a big, bushy mustache, just like I expected from a war hero. My imagination played out scenes of explosions and gunfire, Uncle Taylor tying a bandana around his head before killing large swaths of people with a machine gun.

I unbuckled my seatbelt, climbed in between their seats, and said, "Mom says you're a hero? What did you do?"

"Sit back and buckle your seatbelt young man," said my uncle, while mom flashed me an angry look. I sat back and clicked my seatbelt, defeated.

"My dad has three ladders but you can't use any of them," Carl said to Tony.

"Why?" said Tony.

"Because he said so," Carl snapped.

"You can't run off a ladder anyway," said Tony.

"Bees will hurt you. Leave them alone," said Tamika.

"Shut up Tamika," Cal said.

"Maybe we can find a rock and hit'em," Carl said.

"That'll just make them mad," Tony said.

"How about my ball?" I said, imagining a bee or two getting trapped inside the wiffle ball, coming down to us, being our friend.

"That might work," Tony said.

I sprinted back to Uncle Taylor's house. I fell through the front door and landed on a woven rug. I looked up. Mom was looking at me from the couch with puffy eyes.

"Do not. Run. In this house," she said, before jumping up, stomping to the bathroom and slamming the door.

I locked eyes with Uncle Taylor while getting up from the floor. He waved me on, then walked over and put his ear to the bathroom door.

I searched my closet for the ball. I found it, held it up to the light and studied my brave probe.

I didn't ask about Uncle Taylor's life as a soldier again, until one day mom and I were cleaning out the garage.

Mom found a dusty shoebox containing old pictures of a young Uncle Taylor. One featured him shirtless, smoking, surrounded by other soldiers, all with dog tags shining in the jungle sun. There was also velvet case inside the shoebox. Mom carefully lifted and opened the case, looked for a moment, then showed it to me. I saw the profile of George Washington etched on a gold heart, attached to a purple ribbon.

"This is a Purple Heart," she said, "They only give it to injured soldiers."

I went to touch it but mom closed the case and put it back in the shoebox.

Later, I found Uncle Taylor, eating macaroni and cheese and flipping through *People* magazine.

"I saw your heart. Your Purple Heart."

"You hear that Michael Jackson got to meet the president? I'll be damned."

"Yeah, Mom told me. How'd you get that medal? What happened?"

"You want some mac'n cheese?"

"No," I said, crossing my arms.

Uncle Taylor looked over my shoulder, sucked his teeth, then looked at the carpet.

He looked up and said, "You finish your chores?"

I began to shake my head.

"Go finish your chores," said Uncle Taylor. He returned to his magazine and his macaroni and cheese.

"Tell me!" I said, hitting the table.

"Finish your chores, young man," he said, in a voice deeper than dad's voice.

I slinked away, defeated.

Wiffle ball in hand, I headed back outside.

"Baby, can you come here," mom said from the living room. My heart sank. I thought she wanted to whoop me for running in the house. I held on to the whiffle ball to signal that I expected to go back outside and play. Mom looked at me from the couch, eyes still puffy.

"Hey, supper is soon. We're having Hamburger Helper."

"Okay. Sounds good, Mom. Are you okay?" I wanted to tell her about the bees to cheer her up, but she might tell me to stay away from them.

"I'm okay baby. Hey, you know your daddy loves you right? He wasn't in the right frame of mind to talk to you. This will make more sense when you're older."

I remembered a picture book dad gave me about insects. In that book, I learned bees have 100 eyes contained in one big eye. I wanted to tell my mother that Dad didn't matter. He'd broken a vow. He lied about me burning up in Arizona. There are bees outside and they have 100 eyes. They are more important than trying to figure out Daddy—that's what I wanted to tell her.

"Okay, Mom. Love you." I said, inching towards the door.

"I love you too baby."

I ran outside, to the palm tree, where Cal and Carl stood under the palm tree fighting over a pair of glasses. I recognized them as X-ray glasses because of the swirled lenses. Cal got them at Showbiz Pizza with Skee-ball tickets.

"Why are you fighting? The glasses don't work." Tony said.

"Yes they do," Cal and Carl said.

Tamika and I giggled at the sight of the twins wrestling each other over plastic glasses.

"One of them says there's honey inside. The other says bee poop in there. Then they fight," laughed Tamika.

I handed Tony the whiffle ball. He studied it and experimented with different grips. The boys stopped wrestling. They looked at Tony, then looked at the beehive, then looked back at Tony. Tony settled on a grip, cocked his arm back, poked his tongue out the side of his mouth, cocked his arm back even further, and threw the ball at the hive. It struck the center of the hive. A dark cloud of bees descended on our heads. We ran as fast as we could.

JOHN LENNON

1

Just ask her. Okay, that sounded okay. She said yes. She's smiling. I bet no one ever invites her to readings. The reading will probably suck. No, don't mention it. Talking about how the reading might suck is a turn off. Say goodbye now. What a smile. Good job. The reading will be okay. It will be boring in parts but Samantha is reading. Samantha's funny. Funny and honest.

2

Shit, should've cleaned my car. Toss the cans in the back. Toss the sweater in the back. Reach under the seat and grab that nasty french fry. Throw that shit out the window. Okay, here she is. Tell her she looks great. Why did my voice crack? Make a joke! Not about puberty! Okay, she laughed. Breathe. Find something on the radio. No Lil Wayne. No John Lennon. Oh shit, she likes John Lennon. Turn it back. John Lennon. This might not work. Tell her that story about how John and Yoko met. Tell her it was at Yoko's art show. Tell her there was a ladder in the middle of the gallery. Tell her at the top of the ladder there was a magnifying glass attached to the ceiling. Tell her that John climbed the ladder. Tell her when John Lennon was at the top of the ladder, he moved the magnifying glass over a tiny word on the ceiling and read, "Yes." What a cool art thing, Yoko! Tell her you don't know if that story is true. Don't tell her that.

Oh, her dad listens to John Lennon. I bet her dad is 7 foot 7. I bet he's a former wrestler-slash-fighter pilot with a huge mustache. Has tattoos. Is racist. What is she talking about now? She's talking too fast. Whole Foods? Ask her to say that again. Hey, what's this guy doing! Jesus Christ! Okay, breathe. Apologize. Ask if she's okay. What the hell? Walking in the middle of the street, at night, in all black. Maybe he wanted to die. Maybe he just left a reading. She's not talking. What were we talking about? Her dad. Ask her about her dad. No, she was talking about Whole Foods or something. Ask her about Whole Foods. Oh, someone works at Whole Foods. Seems like a cool job. Benefits. Is she talking about her ex? Yep. It's her ex. Mike. Great, he's a filmmaker. A filmmaker who works at Whole Foods.

3

Do people like this? He's still reading. In a western shirt. That girl is checking her phone. I'm going to check my phone. What will people think if I check my phone? Maybe it's an important text. Shit, he stopped reading. I should clap. Where do I put my beer? It's hard to clap with this beer. I'm not producing sound with this clap. I'm showing approval by pretending to clap. I think he saw me fake clap. What if he ripped off his western shirt, got in my face? Jesus, could I fight? Hope I never have to fist-fight.

What is she doing? Cool, yes, meet you back here. Is there anyone I wouldn't hate small talk with? Samantha is talking to western shirt guy. Just tell her you don't want to interrupt, but you like the poem with the cat and the cliffs. Don't go on and on. Don't tell her you thought the reading might suck. Damn, she just walked away. Western shirt guy was too much. Not too late to change course myself. I'll just stand here alone. Look at people. There's that girl that checked her phone. I'm going to check my phone.

Good, she's back. She looks good. Try to mime looking through a magnifying glass like John Lennon. Tilt your head up. I don't think she got it.

Yes. I do want to get out of here.

4

Another Mike story? Just wish her a good night and drive away. Shit, I missed her turn. She's laughing. Laugh with her. She said she liked the reading. That she had a good time. So everything's cool. Just friends. Okay, turn right here. There's her house. Just thank her for coming out. Maybe a hug. Okay, kiss. Yeah, this is good too. These are nice lips.

This is happening. Do I want to go in? Say no. Say you're tired. Just say yes. We can do this. Just breathe. Jesus, all these plants. She loves plants. Nice place. I'll just sit down here. Okay, breathe. Bookshelf. Zadie. Packer. Introduction to Black Studies. Harry Potter, volume one through a million.

Ha! What's up little dog? Just peeping through the window? Can't let you in buddy. She's going to come out soon. She's going to be disappointed. Samantha was great tonight. Her poem was like:

> *a house*
> *atop a high cliff*
> *alone, or with a cat*

Oh well. She's calling me to the bedroom. Here we go. You can do this. This won't be like how it was with Jamie. Or Elaine. Or Sheila. You're an adult now. Just focus. Her lips are nice. She's taking off her shirt. Take off your shirt. Does she have a condom? Do I ask for one? She's taking off her jeans. Take off your jeans. Kiss her neck. Kiss her breasts. She must be reaching for a condom. I'm not there yet.

What was that? Who is knocking on the fucking door? Who is calling her name? Mike? Who the fuck is Mike? Oh right. Great. Of course. This was a huge mistake. Don't shush me. I'm not saying shit. I wonder if he'll come in here. I'll have to fistfight him. Naked. Breathe. She's calm. She knows him. Knows he'll just go away. Just be silent. Seems like he's gone. She had it under control. No one's whispered *shhh* in my ear since I was little. Still tickles from her breath. That was nice. She looks nice. Mood's ruined though. I just want to pet her dog and go.

THE
BILLY PROBLEM

BILLY IS ON A BUS. HE'S GOING TO VISIT HIS grandmother. We don't know why Billy is going to visit his grandmother. Maybe he visits to help her vacuum and dust the China hutch?

Maybe Billy's grandmother has poor eyesight and he reads aloud her favorite scriptures? Maybe he reads her the news because she refuses to watch television?

Maybe every Saturday (if it is Saturday) he mows his grandmother's yard with a rusted push mower from 1950-something and every two or three feet the grass has to be pulled out of the mower by hand, turning his fingers neon green?

We can assume Billy likes his grandmother, or at least feels an obligation towards her, because he's going to her house. Or maybe she lives in an assisted living facility that smells like molded oatmeal?

But we don't know.

By looking at Billy's face, we don't know how he feels about visiting his grandmother. His face does not appear contented, annoyed, distressed, or bored. Can we tell how Billy feels from whether he looks out the window, at graffiti on the bus seat, at a crushed M&M on the bus floor, or at another passenger's hat?

Maybe Billy's grandmother, at times, forgets Billy is her grandson. Maybe he's looking out the bus window and hoping that today is a day she remembers. Maybe he does these things for his grandmother because she's the only mother Billy has known. Honestly, we don't know.

The only thing we know is Billy is on a bus. He is going to visit his grandmother. His face is neither contented, annoyed, distressed or bored.

Is Billy's face a young face? Is it a white face? Is it an Asian face? Maybe his face is Black? We don't know. We only know that looking at Billy's face is an unreliable way to determine his true feelings about the bus, about his grandmother, or taking the bus to go see his grandmother.

We may imagine Billy listening to the bus's brakes and adjusting his body in the seat. We may imagine the graffiti on the bus seat says "CARL" or a nearby passenger has a bright purple hat.

We may imagine Billy fixating on the crushed M&M on the bus floor and not thinking about his grandmother, who, we may imagine, may've asked him, the last time he visited, "Who are you? Why are you in my house?" Again, we can imagine, but we don't know.

There is something we do know: "Billy" is a play on "Bill," which is short for "William." What we don't know is if his birth certificate says "William" or simply "Billy." We don't know if William was the name of Billy's grandfather, who may or may not have died of a stroke while washing his Lincoln Navigator at a self-service car wash. We don't know if they found Billy's grandfather on the wet concrete floor, mouth and nose full of suds. We just know someone decided to call Billy "Billy" and that he, for some reason, decided to get on a bus to visit his grandmother.

MODERN MASSACRES

ALEX SWIPES HIS CREDIT CARD ON THE TOUCH screen device, places his card in his wallet, then puts his wallet in his pocket.

The touch screen asks him to *hold one moment, please*. He sees a blinking ellipsis.

There must be $10,000 of yoga gear in this place, Alex thinks, looking around at yoga mats, yoga pants, yoga headbands, and water bottles with *yoga is life* written on the side.

The touch screen beeps and displays the word "error."

"Um, it's a chip reader," says the barista.

"Oops," Alex says, glancing meekly at the line behind him.

Alex takes out his wallet, removes his credit card, and inserts it chip-side up. The ellipsis appears then disappears quickly before asking him for a tip. He taps "10%" and signs his name by running his finger across the screen. He walks to a table near a window and sits.

He pictures a white man in a tan suit and red tie, sitting cross-legged, staring intently at him, explaining in a British drawl, "The move from card-swiping to chip-reading happened years ago. And while the transition in the United States left something to be desired, you're still an idiot and everyone here knows it." The man waves a hand in the air to indicate "everyone."

Everyone here knows it, Alex thinks to himself, fighting the urge to look at people's faces for confirmation. He imagines the yoga-loving strangers' faces pointed at him, demanding with hateful voices that he be removed from the coffee shop.

He remembers a psychologytoday.com article he read last week titled *5 Tips for Managing Social Anxiety*.

Number One, Alex thinks, *You can't control what people think of you*.

Alex takes out *Modern Massacres* by S.P. Anderson, a book the famous historian Richard

Domination called "a dark but necessary catalogue of state-sponsored murder." His partner Shelly wanted to clean their apartment, to dust the fiddle-leaf fig and vacuum the floor, and so she shooed him out. He jammed the book in a tote and headed for the new coffee shop.

Before *Modern Massacres*, he'd read *Labor Camp* by VI Sakharov at a pace that gave him nightmares. Sometimes he'd drift off at night and find himself shivering in a Soviet labor camp, in the stinging cold, taking a bite of hard black bread and tucking the rest into the tattered lining of his coat. Just as a gang boss prepared to beat him up for hiding bread, he'd wake up, with perfect vision in the dark, still sensing the cold as Shelly snored quietly next to him. One day, while reading a passage about what happened to a woman who tried to escape the camp (they left her corpse by the wall as a warning), Shelly asked him for help carrying in the groceries. "I'm doing something," he snapped at her. They didn't speak for the whole evening. Just before bed they had a small fight about who does the grocery shopping. They agreed he needed to take a break from reading about labor camps. Now he's reading, slowly, a book about state-sponsored murder.

Alex waits for his $4 coffee and thinks warmly of Shelly singing Mariah Carey songs while carefully dusting the leaves of their large fiddle-leaf fig, which they named Dolly. At their old apartment, Dolly's big leaves were deep green and pointed upward. In their new place, the leaves turned lime and drooped. *She seems fine to me*, Alex remembers saying, pointing to three or four new sprouts, but the color change continued to worry Shelly. She spent a lot of time examining Dolly, moving her around the living room, stroking her leaves, singing *We Belong Together* to her. He imagines blowing Shelly's mind by waving his hand over Dolly and Dolly's leaves becoming deep green again. He imagines restoring entire rainforests with his new-found superpowers. His daydream is interrupted by the sight of three men with haircuts and zero body fat walking by, yoga mats slung across their chests with hemp rope. Alex wonders at the lightness and symmetry of their bodies, and considers his own flabbiness, how his mid-body stacks like pancakes.

"ALEX. Iced Americano. For ALEX."

Alex walks towards the counter. The man in the tan suit stands up and says, "Who is this nigger in our coffee shop? With his ignorance of our payment methods, his flabby body, his grotesque literature?"

Alex ignores the man, picks up the mason jar full of coffee from the counter, and nods at the barista. He sits and begins reading about the K Massacre. The K Massacre started when a dictator occupied an adjacent country. The dictator thought the capital of the occupied country—the city of K— was full of spies. The dictator's secret police arrested 15,000 people in the city and shot them.

Four dollars for iced coffee? Alex thinks, *Well, 15,000 people got fucking shot, buddy. Think about that. 15,000 people gone in a couple of months.*

Alex opens his notebook and writes "K Massacre" in block letters. He sips his straw but the mason jar is empty and the slurp echoes throughout the coffee shop. A woman in a shirt that reads "Yoga. Coffee. Naps." glances at Alex before going back to her phone.

Number Two. You can't control what people think of you.

Alex focuses on the book. There was a little room where the secret police confirmed your identity by forcing you to name your relatives. Then, they blindfolded you and walked you to a different room, which was soundproofed to mute the shot. Then, your body was carried off and dumped in a mass grave. He thinks of how the executioners worked in shifts, took lunch breaks and got weekends off. He imagines them drinking coffee and complaining about a sick fiddle leaf fig.

Alex watches a couple in matching "I haven't had my ~~Coffee~~ Yoga" shirts struggle to control a clumsy labradoodle. He thinks about how he would confess to anything the secret police wanted. He senses himself worrying that, for the crime of slurping his drink, the woman in the "Yoga. Coffee. Naps." shirt would report him to the secret police.

You can't control what people think of you.

Alex senses the man in the tan suit staring more intensely now. He thinks, *When genocide happens there is always someone, somewhere, slurping expensive coffee.* He packs up his book and leaves the coffee shop. He looks down the street, where he sees more people carrying yoga mats and wearing yoga pants. They all seem to be marching in step with each other, like a yoga army, invading the neighborhood, raising the price of coffee beans and driving ethnic minorities from their homes.

Once home, he admires Shelly's work. The pillows are straight on the couch, the chairs are angled just-so, the record player is dust free and the blinds in the bay window are evenly drawn so the right amount of light hits Dolly. He plops on the couch and begins reading, then puts the book down and stares at Dolly's leaves.

She seems fine.

He imagines a citizen of K, a man, lying down on a couch in a well-ordered apartment, the top button of his shirt unfastened, staring at a fiddle-leaf fig in questionable health, never in a million years imagining that soon he'll end up in a tiny room, naming his relatives.

Shelly enters the room and approaches Dolly slowly. He begins telling her about the K Massacre, about how weird it is that mass murder is something considered and designed.

Shelly sighs in a resigned way, before stroking Dolly's leaves and saying, "I wish I knew what was wrong with you."

LITERARY PARTIES IN METROPOLITAN CITIES

I WAS BORED SO I ASKED TOM, A NOVELIST who'd been shortlisted for the Booker Prize the year before, if he wanted to do drugs.

"Hell yeah," Tom said.

I looked around the room. I saw that James, a National Book Award-winning memoirist, was sweating and talking frantically to a Walt Whitman Award-winning poet named Valerie. He was clearly on drugs.

Tom and I walked over to them. I asked him where I could find some MDMA. He looked annoyed and said, "I have some, but I don't have any capsules so we have to snort it."

"No problem, how much?"

The *New Yorker* 30 Under 30 novelist Mark White appeared and said, "It's free if you snort it off my ass."

James said, "Fuck yeah."

I looked at Tom and said, "Okay."

We walked to the bathroom.

James sat on the toilet and took out a baggie of powder. James' latest book was about his travels with a group of refugees. He made millions of dollars.

Mark, Tom, and I stepped into the bathtub.

Tom said it was weird how we all got in the bathtub instinctively. Tom wrote a small but powerful novel about a man who becomes addicted to playing *Call of Duty* on Xbox and ruins his life.

James stood and said, "Drop them draws."

Mark pulled down his pants and underwear and pointed his ass at Tom and I. I resisted looking at Mark's ass but then decided to look at it. Mark, being of Irish descent, wrote a series of novels about the Ulster Massacres in 1641. His ass was pale as paper with black tufts of hair coming from his crack.

"Mark White's white-ass ass." I thought to myself, picturing the words appearing in *New Yorker* cartoon font.

James moved closer to Mark with the baggie in hand. The bathroom door opened and he pulled back.

Jessica and Hillary, both finalists for the Tuft Poetry Awards, stumbled in and looked at us standing in the bathtub.

Hillary giggled and said, "What the fuck are you guys doing?"

James said, "Shut the door."

I said, "We're snorting MDMA off Mark's ass."

Jessica's book of poems, *Moored Vessel*, is an examination of the year she spent paralyzed in bed and suffering from a rare disease. She said, "Hell yeah," and slapped Mark's ass.

Hillary's book of poems, *Matza and Gritz*, is a journey into the life of a black Jew growing up in the deep south. Mark looked at Hillary and said, "Matza and MDMA on my ass." Everyone except Hillary laughed.

Tom said, "Can we hold on for a second? I have to call my wife."

Everyone paused. We looked at each other, unsure how to respond. Tom's wife went by one name, all caps, "LIGHT." She won a Hugo Boss Prize for sculpture.

Tom called her and asked, "Honey, can I snort MDMA off Mark White's ass?"

We fell silent, wondering what Tom's wife would say. My stomach groaned loud enough for everyone to hear. I clutched it. As I was about to apologize, Tom said, "Thank you honey, I love you too."

Tom put his phone away and gave us a thumbs up. We all cheered.

James positioned himself behind Mark and tipped the baggie over Mark's lower back.

I felt the urge to say, "That's his lower back, not his ass," but there was no way James could move the powder to Mark's ass.

James separated the powder into lines on Mark's lower back with a gold credit card.

Mark, facing the corner where the beige tiles converged, said "Tickles," causing a little echo.

Tom handed me a rolled-up bill. I took the bill and leaned towards Mark's ass. I sniffed a line off of Mark's lower back while thinking, "This is not Mark's ass, this is his lower back."

I stepped out of the bathtub and handed the bill to Tom. He moved his face toward Mark's ass and sniffed a line off of Mark's lower back.

Mark looked back at Tom and said, "Your wife would be proud."

OFFICER WALTER

1

We just finished sliding into our desks when a police officer entered the classroom with a briefcase.

Mrs. Riley beamed at us like she'd brought us Pizza Hut.

The police officer set his briefcase on Mrs. Riley's desk.

"Kids, my name is Officer Walter. I'm with the Drug Abuse Resistance Program. Mrs. Riley has invited me to talk to you about the dangers of drugs."

Jerry and James pointed at Officer Walter's gun. It was shiny, black and attached to his hip. Officer

Walter smiled and opened the briefcase. Mrs. Riley motioned for us to gather around her desk. Inside the briefcase, we saw a baggie with white powder, a baggie with yellow powder, colorful squares of paper, a pill bottle, a syringe, and a greenish-brown leaf.

Officer Walter pointed with his index and middle fingers to the baggie with white powder.

"That's cocaine!" gasped Libby Anderson. Officer Walter raised his eyebrows.

"That's right," he said, stiffening and putting his hands behind his back. "Just one sniff and you'll be stealing money for your $700-a-day habit."

Libby gasped again.

"And that's marijuana," Office Walter said, pointing to the leaf. "Just one puff can make you violent and lazy."

I looked at the crosshatched lines on his gun's handle. I wanted to ask him if he'd ever shot someone for having marijuana. I saw a man get caught with marijuana on the TV show COPS. He ran and the cops shot him. The man dropped to the ground. He rolled over and looked toward the camera. The man's face and wounds were blurred.

"This is acid. Kids, it will fry your brain," he said, pointing to the square of paper.

Libby gasped again.

2

Mom invited Officer Walter over for dinner. My stepfather was deployed to Saudi Arabia, so Officer Walter sat at the head of the table. His gun was black, like his jeans, and attached neatly to his belt loop.

Mom told him she liked her job at Melvyn's, but that she wanted to join the police force.

"Is that crazy?" she asked, touching Officer Walter's shoulder. "That must be crazy."

"It's a dangerous profession," he said, leaning towards her. "But you might have what it takes."

"You think so?"

"Yeah, written test, couple weeks of training. You're in."

They went on to talk about me. She said I was a good young man. She said I didn't talk with an accent or sag my pants.

"He has respect. And a sense of responsibility," she said.

She went to pet my head but pulled her hand back just before her fingertips reached my brow.

"He better," said Officer Walter, "or else I'll have to crack his head." He made his right hand into a small fist and punched his left palm.

They laughed.

I thought about my stepdad, who said a similar thing to me before he left for Saudi Arabia.

"Respect your Mom while I'm away, or else I'll crack your head," he said.

3

I pulled the chair from under Chucky Alvarado when he went to sit. He fell to the floor and chipped his tooth. I laughed. James and Jerry laughed too but in a muted way. Chucky was holding his mouth in pain. He looked at me with glassy eyes and walked out of the classroom. A minute later, Mr. Geary walked in and started Music class. Chucky didn't come back.

After school, we usually played basketball in Terrence Smith's driveway. It was strange not seeing Chucky there. James asked about him.

"He chipped his tooth. His daddy is making him come kick yo ass," said Terrence, pointing at me and laughing. Jerry and James laughed too.

I shrugged, shot the ball, missed.

We played three on three. Halfway through the game, James said, "Hey, there's Chucky." Everyone paused to watch him walk towards us. I kept dribbling the ball around, shooting and missing.

Chucky walked right up to me. I didn't look at him or say anything. I kept dribbling.

"You chipped my tooth. Now my daddy has to pay for it," Chucky said.

A crowd formed around us. It was impossible to ignore what was happening. He was there to fight me.

"What, I—" but before I could finish, Chucky punched me in the eye. My face exploded with pain. Everything went black. I cupped my eye socket and began crying in front of everyone. I ran home.

I told my mother what happened. She gave me a disappointed look and said, "I'm calling Officer Walter." I begged her not to, but she insisted.

Officer Walter arrived in blue jeans, gun holstered on his hip. He asked mom for a notepad and pen. Mom handed them to Officer Walter. He turned to me and asked for a statement.

"What is a statement?" I asked, thinking I had to fill out some paperwork.

Officer Walter glanced at mom. "Your story. What happened?"

I told him.

He smiled and tossed the notepad and pen on the table. The pen rolled off the table and onto the floor. He ignored it. He told me he had to discuss the investigation privately with my mother. He undid the holster and set his gun on our kitchen table. He told me to wait here while they went upstairs.

I watched as he followed Mom upstairs.

I stared at Officer Walter's gun on the table. I poked it with my finger and got excited. I wanted to pick it up. I looked at the stairs and looked back at the gun. I picked it up. My hand wasn't used to the weight and my knuckles wrapped the table. I got a handle on it and took it out of the holster. I pointed the gun at the ceiling. I pointed it at the TV. I pointed it at the fridge. I jumped from behind the corner and pointed the gun at the cat. The cat ran upstairs. I put the gun to my forehead. I laughed and noticed the notepad on the table. I put the gun back in the holster. I picked up the pen and set it on the table. I opened the notepad to read my statement. The pages were empty.

4

Mom's office was in Women's Apparel at Melvyn's, behind a door partially concealed by mirrored column. On her desk were lots of carbon copy receipts and returned merchandise, including about 12 Swatch watches. I told Jerry the watches had been there for weeks. Jerry said I should take them. He said no one would miss them. I wanted the green watch with yellow and blue triangles in the face. He wanted the blue watch with squiggly yellow arms and purple squares for numbers.

I put the two watches in my pocket and met Jerry in the food court. I gave him the blue watch and kept the green watch. We put them on and checked them several times on the way to the arcade. They were dead, but looked cool on our arms.

I heard mom call my name. She'd travelled deep into the mall to find me. She was wearing her nametag.

"Both of you. Follow me."

Jerry ripped off the blue watch and threw it at me. It bounced off my stomach and fell to the ground. I picked it up and watched Jerry run away. I started walking behind my mother. I followed to a large office behind Electronics at Melvyn's. We sat in chairs in front of a large desk. She stared at the space in front of her.

A thin white man with black-rimmed glasses sat at the desk. I recognized him as mom's boss, Steve. Officer Walter walked in a few moments later. I looked at his gun. It was a silver revolver with a black handle.

"I understand we have a shoplifting case," said Steve, looking over his glasses at my mother.

"Yes sir. He thought he could get away with it," said my mother, shaking her head and looking at Steve.

"I'm sorry," I said, hanging my head.

"That merchandise was property of Melvyn's incorporated son, you had no right to take it. You stole from me and your mother, and every employee in this store," Steve said, leaning back in his chair.

He looked over his glasses at Officer Walter, "Officer Walter, if I press charges, how much jail time is that?"

"At least 20 to 30 months," Officer Walter said, tilting his head at me.

I imagined sleeping on the floor of a prison cell and began crying.

"I'm so sorry. I promise I won't do it again."

"You'd better not," Steve said.

I saw mom look at the ceiling and shake her head.

5

I was walking down the street and a cop pulled up beside me. The cop told me to stop. He got out of his cruiser. I wanted to tell him that mom tried to become a cop. I wanted to tell him that she failed the written test. I wanted to tell him I knew Officer Walter. He asked me for ID. I told him I was fourteen and didn't have an ID. He took out handcuffs and told me to put my hands behind my back. I did as I was told. He squeezed the cuffs on tight, grabbed my wrist and walked me to the cop car. I did as I was told. He bent me over the car. The hood was hot and my chest tingled with pain.

The cop left me there, bent over the car. Pain covered my chest and began to pulse in my wrists. I watched him talk into his walkie-talkie for a minute or two, then Officer Walter pulled up. He said something to the cop and motioned towards me. Officer Walter looked at me and shook his head before driving away.

The cop walked back over to me, lifted me off the car and unlocked the handcuffs.

"You fit a description," he said, before getting in his car and driving away. I walked home, rubbing my wrists.

6

Libby overdosed on cocaine and had a seizure. Her boyfriend Jerry wanted to visit her in the hospital, but her dad said no. To cheer Jerry up, I stole my stepdad's case of Bud Light and mom's minivan. I drove with Jerry and James to a house party in a neighboring town.

About an hour in, Jerry was screaming at different people at the party. He tried to fight Nathan Orville when Nathan asked about Libby. When Jerry passed out on the porch, James and I decided to take him home. We grabbed what was left of the Bud Light, carried Jerry to the minivan, and put down the seats. He collapsed in the back, knocking away empty Bud Light cans. James put the box with the remaining beers next to Jerry.

James put on Bone Thugs and we started singing along. I rolled down the window and sang into the hay-scented wind. I started singing louder and driving faster.

We heard a siren. Lights lit up the minivan cabin. James turned down the music. I looked in the rearview and saw the black and white car. I looked back at Jerry and saw the box of beer and the empty cans.

"We're going to fucking jail dude," said James.

I got out my license. The cop kept his lights on the side mirror. All I could see were his cop shoes. When he got to my window, I recognized Officer Walter.

"License and registration please. Do you know how fast you were going?"

"No sir," I said, handing him my license and registration. His gun was dark gray and eye level with me.

"45 in a 30, son," he said, looking at my license. He pointed his flashlight at Jerry, who was snoring amongst the empty cans, then he put the flashlight in my face.

"Do you want me to crack your head, son?"

"No, sir," I said. *We're going to fucking jail*, I thought.

"Well then slow down and get that boy home safe, okay?" Officer Walter said, pointing to Jerry in the back seat.

"Yes sir," I said.

"Tell your mother I said..." Officer Walter started. He shook his head. "Never mind."

He waved us off. I put away my license and registration. I pulled out carefully. Once we were a little down the road, James and I began howling with laughter and relief. Jerry woke up, yelled, "Take me to the fucking hospital. I gotta see her," and passed out again.

7

Vanilla told me he was drinking rubbing alcohol in his Sonic Cherry Limeade. I called bullshit.

"Man, look," he said, lifting up his shirt. I thought I'd fucked up. I'd heard Vanilla had once gotten drunk at party and started hacking at random people with a machete. I let out a nervous giggle when he produced a bottle of rubbing alcohol. He twisted off the cap with his mouth. He poured a couple drops into the limeade, swirled it with the straw, and took a big pull, cap still in his mouth.

"You're crazy, man," I said, laughing, "That shit is poison."

Just then someone yelled, "Cops are here!"

Vanilla disappeared.

Everyone rushed for the door, turning Mike's kitchen into a bottleneck.

After a few chaotic moments, I heard Officer Walter's voice.

"Calm down, everyone. We just need you vacate the premises."

I made it outside, where James stood by the minivan.

"Where's Jerry?"

"He's talking to Libby," James said, pointing over my shoulder. I turned to see Vanilla, Jerry and Libby standing under a large magnolia.

Jerry was shaking his head at Libby.

I heard Officer Walter's voice again.

"*Hold up.* I need everyone to stay where they are." He held a small baggie of white powder up with tweezers. I saw Libby patting her pockets. She looked at Jerry and Jerry mimed something angrily at her.

"Everyone line up for a search," Officer Walter said.

Vanilla, Jerry, Libby and three of Vanilla's friends bolted down the street. A cop yelled, "We got runners!" and all the cops but Officer Walter ran after them. Speaking into his walkie-talkie, Officer Walter told the dispatcher that Vanilla was a white male with red hair running eastward on Carlson Street.

Once Office Walter finished, he realized that all the other cops had run off. He looked around nervously. His hand was resting on his gun so I couldn't see it.

"Everyone stay here," Officer Walter yelled. He pointed to several random spots on the ground and galloped backwards. He looked directly at me and repeated, "Stay here." He turned and ran eastward on Carlson Street.

James and I got in the minivan and drove west on Carlson Street.

CHEERLEADERS

"BITCH, WAKE YO ASS UP," KEVIN SAID, SLAP-ping Matt's forehead.

"I'm not asleep," Matt said, holding his forehead.

Kevin turned to Luke and said, "Are these girls even coming?"

Luke, who was leaning over the coffee table, singing along to *Bone Thugs-in-Harmony* and carefully hollowing out a Phillies Blunt, hunched his shoulders and frowned.

"I just talked to them. They're coming," Jason said. He glanced out the patio window and shook his head.

"I don't think they're coming," Kevin said.

"I called Erin," Jason said. "They said they'd be here soon."

"I got dibs on Jessica," Kevin said.

"We'll see about that, homie," Luke said, sprinkling dry weed in the wet blunt paper.

While watching Luke press the blunt paper around the weed, Matt pictured Erin, Jessica, and Stacy cheering in their cheerleading uniforms.

No way they come over. Especially Stacy. She's a good girl, Matt thought.

He remembered when Mr. Herbert dropped his pencil in Spanish class. Matt said "d'oh" like Homer Simpson and Stacy looked back at him and giggled over her shoulder.

"I got dibs on Stacy," Matt said. Kevin and Jason laughed.

Luke said, "Go for the gold, homie," and licked the length of the blunt.

Matt looked at the carpet, stained and matted in places.

"Yo where's the vodka? Let's take shots," Kevin said, punching his palm.

Jason reached into a paper bag and pulled out a big plastic jug of vodka. He held the bottle up and said, "Gahhhhhh."

Jeff appeared from the kitchen with five plastic cups featuring the Godfather's Pizza logo: an Italian man in a pinstripe suit smoking a cigar over a pizza.

Jason handed Godfather cups of Smirnoff to Matt, Jason, and Kevin, before taking one himself.

Matt downed his shot. He tried to hold back the urge to retch. He moved his tongue around his mouth to rid himself of the aftertaste. Kevin and Jeff took their shots and their faces contorted.

Struck with the urge to pee, he walked to the bathroom.

We're so lucky Jeff's mom and Stephanie are not here, he thought. He looked at all the dirty clothes on the bathroom floor. *Why don't they pick this shit up?* he thought, *My mom would never allow the bathroom to look like this.* He saw a pair of pink underwear he knew belonged to Stephanie, Jeff's sister. He picked up the underwear with his fingertips. He cringed when he noticed a dark red streak on them. He tossed them into the corner and buried them under a t-shirt and a pair of balled-up jeans.

Cheerleaders, dude, cheerleaders are coming over, he thought, as he began to pee. He heard the door open and voices in the living room. *Oh shit, it's happening.* He finished peeing and flushed the toilet. Walking though the hallway, he recognized Valerie's voice, and thought, *Oh no what the fuck is she doing here.* He entered the living room and saw Valerie talking to Kevin.

"Just give me a shot and a hit and I'll go, promise," said Valerie, glancing at Matt and smiling.

Matt looked at Valerie's half-shaved head. He looked at her purple lipstick and her eyebrow ring. *Why are you so freaky*, he thought.

"Fine, then you gotta bounce," said Kevin.

Everyone took a chair at the dining room table. Luke lit the blunt while Jason put a swig of Smirnoff into everyone's cup. Matt grabbed and drank it quickly. He anticipated retching but only burped. He looked at Valerie's half-shaved head. He remembered how, last year, she took him into the handicapped bathroom and showed him her breasts. He remembered them falling from her hole-ridden *The Cure* t-shirt like two floppy water balloons. They didn't look anything like breasts in movies. He remembered backing out of the bathroom while Valerie looked at him, then looked at her breasts in the mirror, then looked back at him.

Kevin passed Valerie the blunt. She tilted her head back and looked at Matt. He saw her eyes water and watched as she coughed out a plume of smoke.

Ugh is she okay, Matt thought, seeing her slightly hunched over and hacking into the table.

He imagined the cheerleaders walking in, seeing Valerie, and running out in disgust.

"Okay, you've got to go," Matt said.

"Fine. Fine. Jesus. You guys have hot dates?" Valerie said.

"Erin, Jessica, and Stacy are coming over," Matt blurted.

Valerie threw her head back and laughed. "Ugh, those stuck up bitches. I'm out."

Valerie disentangled her wallet chain from the chair and walked to the door.

"Bye," Matt said.

Valerie, without looking back, flipped them off and closed the door.

"Bye," Kevin said in a high-pitched voice.

"Fuck you," Matt said.

"Yo, Matt is that your girl?" Jason said.

"Fuck you," Matt said.

"He hit that in the handicapped bathroom," Kevin said.

"Nah, she just showed him her tits. Matt's a virgin," Jason said, laughing.

"Fuck you," Matt said again, fighting off dizziness. "I'm fucked up."

"Well, get your shit together, homie" Luke said, "Your girlfriend Stacy will be here soon."

Kevin and Jeff laughed.

Matt sat on the couch and felt dizzy again. He looked out the patio door and through the courtyard. *Does mom know I do drugs*, he wondered. *Of course not, she has no idea*, he thought, listening to Kevin as he rapped along to Do or Die's *Po Pimp*.

"Paper Chase is my jam. Paper Chase is better," Matt said, reaching for the Aiwa CD player.

"Don't touch that shit, homie," Luke said, slapping Matt's hand away. Matt pulled his hand back then tried to regain his balance.

"Yeah, let it play," Kevin said.

"Yeah, let it play," Matt mocked.

Kevin looked at Matt and said, "Bitch."

"What are you going to do," Matt said, stabbing a finger at Kevin.

Matt heard giggling outside. He saw everyone in the room freeze and stare at the door. He heard a faint knock and watched as Jeff walked to the door.

This is gonna be tough, Matt thought.

Jeff opened the door and Matt saw Erin Lafferty's face. Behind her stood Jessica Borden and Stacy Whitmore. Just as Matt became annoyed with Jeff for not flinging the door open and inviting them in, Jeff flung the door open and said, "Come in."

Matt watched as Erin walked directly to Jason and sat next to him, while Stacy and Jessica looked around nervously.

"Y'all want a drink? We have vodka," Jeff said, holding up the bottle of Smirnoff.

"Hell yeah," Erin said, putting her arms around Jason, squeezing him, and then playfully pushing him away.

Jeff rushed to the kitchen to fill the cups with ice. Stacy and Jessica walked to the far end of the couch and sat on the edge, near Erin. Matt noticed all their knees were close together. Luke pulled the brim of his Notre Dame cap tight around his eyes.

Erin whispered in Jason's ear. They both got up off the couch. Jason led her to the bedroom. Stacy turned and cringed at Jessica. Jessica rolled her eyes, then inched closer to Luke on the couch. Jeff came back with three Godfather cups with vodka.

Kevin looked at Jessica and Stacy and said, "So wassup y'all."

Stacy sighed, looked at Luke, and said, "Nothing."

Jessica took a cup from Jeff and said, "Where's Stephanie?"

"She's in Dallas with my mom. Visiting my uncle," Jeff said.

"Where does your mom live?" Jessica asked.

"She lives here, with me and Stephanie." Jeff said, confused by the question.

"Your mom lives *here*?" Jessica said, looking at the stained, matted carpet.

"Anyone wanna hit this?" Luke said, holding up the half-smoked blunt.

"Oh me, me, me." Matt said in a toddler's voice.

Stacy and Jessica giggled.

"Bro, you're such a bitch," Kevin said.

"Whatever, hoe," Matt said, leaning over to take the blunt from Luke.

Matt took a big hit, held it in his lungs, and passed the blunt to Jeff.

Matt exhaled. A large cloud formed above Jessica and Stacy.

Jessica waved her hand in the air and Stacy began coughing.

"So do they drug test y'all? On the cheerleading team?" Kevin asked.

"No," Jessica said, "Why would they drug test for cheerleading?"

"They do if you're pro," Stacy said.

"Either way, I don't smoke. Smoking is nasty," Jessica said, waving her hand again.

Kevin said, "Yeah, put it out Luke."

Luke shook his head and said, "Fuck that."

Stacy giggled and pushed Luke.

Luke dropped the blunt on the couch. He squealed and picked it up. He watched the cherry fall back into the couch and said, "Fuck."

Matt said "d'oh," like Homer Simpson. He looked at Stacy and laughed.

Stacy stared at the couch with a concerned expression while Luke tried to stamp out the embers with his hand.

Matt's laugh turned into a loud cough. His mouth flooded with saliva. He began coughing and drooling over the side of the couch.

Stacy said, "Um, is he going to be okay?" and pointed at Matt.

Matt nodded, wiped his mouth, and began coughing again. He felt his stomach squeeze itself. Vomit spilled from his throat and splashed on the carpet. Matt knelt on the carpet and vomited again. On his hands and knees, his face pointed at the carpet, drool hanging from his bottom lip, he heard the cheerleaders squeal.

Kevin jumped up and down next to Matt and yelled, "Get your gross ass to the bathroom now!" Matt ran clumsily to the bathroom. He fell to the floor, crawled to the toilet, and propped himself over it while feeling the room spin. He drooled and heard voices and people moving around. He heaved into the toilet. He saw vomit splashing from the toilet onto the pile of clothes that buried Stephanie's underwear.

He fell on the floor, leaned against the bathtub, and took deep breaths as the room kept spinning.

He heard Stephanie's bedroom door open. He heard muffled voices and the front door open. He heard the front door close and the voices fade. The room began to spin faster.

THE MOVIES

1

Pat saw a young woman inspecting tomatoes. She wore gold sandals and cut off shorts. She picked up a tomato, squeezed it with slender fingers, and then placed it down gently, like a chess piece. When she did this with a second tomato, he noticed the scars on her forearm.

Mary? He thought. He looked closer, confirmed it was Mary, then saw her clear eyes land on him and brighten with excitement. He feigned a double take and waved at her, hoping she would casually wave back and continue inspecting tomatoes. She began pushing her cart quickly towards the cheese bin where Pat stood, helpless to stop her.

–Hello! Patrick! Mary hollered, not yet near him. He'd forgotten about her accent. He opened his arms enthusiastically wide, and while leaning into the hug, felt embarrassed by his insincerity.

–Why haven't you called me?

Mary shamed him for his absence, then segued into the meanwhile of her life: her latest argument with Dana, the issues with her Comp Lit program, a trip she took to somewhere for a conference on Gender Studies, and the gold sandals she brought back from that trip.

–Do you like them?

–Yeah, they're pretty. Where did you get them again?

–Montreal. Gender Studies conference. I just told you. Dana hates them. Says they make my ankles look big.

–Oh please, your ankles would snap if you tied them too tight.

Mary smiled, turned pink, and then paled again.

–Come out with me on Saturday. There's a movie playing on campus I really want to see. It's a documentary called *Night Sweats*. It's about a man addicted to prostitutes. Dana won't see it with me.

2

Pat eased his frown. It was forced anyway, to show resolve. Mary's mouth was open. Pat fidgeted on his side of the bed. He repeated himself:

–I'm sorry. I just can't be with someone who does what you do.

Pat smoothed out the sheet between them, making it neat and free of wrinkles. Mary shuffled to the edge of the bed and put her face in her hands.

3

– Yeah, I'll go to the movies with you.

– Good. Call me. It starts at 8.

Mary placed a wheel of brie in her cart and pushed it towards a cluster of checkout lines. Pat watched her walk away and thought *Exhaustion*, if that was what he felt.

4

Mary paired her wrists on Pat's chest. He locked his fingers over the small of Mary's back. He listened to the crickets. The humidity caused window units to click and whir. The motion-sensing light above Mary's garage went out and they were suddenly surrounded by dark. Pat wondered if he was sweating too much.

In the morning, Mary would be in New York City with her ex-boyfriend Marco. As a send-off, they ate chicken enchiladas and watched *Frasier* reruns. Pat waited until he was outside to say goodnight and goodbye. When he approached her for a hug, she folded herself in his arms.

Pat closed his eyes and listened to the crickets alternate songs—one would sing and then the other, and then all of them sang together, but in grinding, shrill chirps. He listened to the chirps absently and worried Mary felt disgusted by the moisture on his chest and armpits. She stretched out her arms, unlocking his fingers. His arms fell to his sides helplessly, like shoelaces cast apart. The motion-sensing light above the garage snapped on and the crickets fell quiet.

–There's something you should know about me. But I'll email you about it when I'm in New York.

–What is it?

–No, it's better if you read it.

–Are you still with Marco?

–No. I've told you that.

Pat pulled his lips into his mouth, trying to summon a better guess, and hoping he wouldn't have to apologize for the first one.

–You can tell me.

−No, it's better if you read it.

Mary inched backwards, towards her front door. The crickets began to chirp. Pat craned his neck up to the dark sky.

5

They were lying in her bed, talking about a professor who had touched her breast. She made scoffing noises through her nose. Pat called the professor a piece of shit, then the conversation lulled. They listened to Brenton Wood's "I'm The One Who Knows." They started whistling the song together, playfully knocking feet. On impulse, Pat ran his fingertips over the scars on her forearm and asked:

−Where did these come from?

Mary raised her arm slowly and wiped at the scars three times, hard and quick like she was trying to brush them away. She sat up and made a fart sound with her mouth. Pat, who took the fart sound personally, wondered if he was prying: they'd only been seeing each other for a week. She told him about Marco.

−My ex. He did it. I mean, I did it, but he did it.

She giggled nervously and made another fart sound.

—So why are you staying in New York with this guy?

—That was a while ago. We're still friends.

Pat looked down at a loose thread hanging from his pillow.

—If you don't know the scars are there, you can barely see them.

—Liar. It's hideous. Dana told me last week that I had the arm of a mental person.

—Don't listen to Dana. It's not that bad. Seriously.

Mary kissed him, bounced up from the bed, and asked if he wanted anything to drink. He said no and grinned at the thread.

Brenton Wood sang:

> *They fly away to a far off land*
> *And live a life that's really grand*

6

—Just tell me now. Don't let me go home with this on my mind.

Mary crossed her arms. The crickets chirped. Her mouth let out a little sigh and her eyes bounced around the street until finally they settled on Pat.

—I'm a foreign student, and I can't work off campus. And I can't support my lifestyle with university money. So I became an escort.

7

Pat massaged the *Night Sweats* program as he read.

—'The true story of a man addicted to prostitutes for twenty years of his life.' Sounds interesting. The director will be here for a Q and A after the film.

—I know. I told you all this. You're just trying to change the subject.

—No, I'm not.

—Yes. You are.

He folded the program and considered the maturity of another denial.

—I'm just saying, strip clubs are just a way to celebrate birthdays. We go maybe two or three times a year.

—Birthdays have nothing to do with it. Nothing. You know that.

—All I'm saying …

—You're saying you objectify women in a disgusting way but don't feel bad about it because your friends are doing it too?

Pat bristled. He watched her glare at the dancing movie snacks painted above the box office. He could've said no to this, not called her, but what would he say if he ran into her at the grocery store again? He stood on his toes to gauge the forward length of the line. He turned to see how far the line extended. He saw a teenager with big ears and freckles making spit bubbles with his mouth. There was no telling how long they'd be there. He tried again.

—I'm sorry. It's just innocent fun.

Mary moved slightly away from Pat. He wanted to reach for her, but he felt like his hand would go right through her body. Pat began to worry strangers would start to assume he was alone. The line moved, tottering the heads in front of them. They took two steps towards the box office before Pat tried again.

—Listen. Truth is I never have much fun. The music is pretty obnoxious. Some of the guys are really weird.

8

Mary took the bus downtown to meet Dana at *Water*, a bar with lime green walls, fiberglass floors and lots of modern furniture. Dana, drunk on Grey Goose, rummaged through her purse and pulled out the card of a campus therapist. Dana said Mary had a problem with men and a poor sense of self-worth.

Later, Mary explained the conversation with Pat. She spoke in a slow, clear voice, as if she were issuing a warning.

–She said my neck is getting fat.

–That another chin is forming.

–She said my hair makes me look like a dyke.

–She said that I'd never find love because I like black men.

–She said I'm faking it in school because I don't really know what to do with my life.

–She said I'm stupid for going to see Marco. That he hasn't changed a bit.

–She said being a whore isn't progressive or interesting, it's just being a whore.

Pat shook his head to show her he disagreed. He had no real opinion of Dana, other than thinking nothing should be that cruel or white. But now Dana served a purpose, bring her up and Mary comes back.

–Why didn't Dana come?

–She said she didn't want to see a movie about whores.

–Does she not know?

–Oh, I've stopped being an escort. Can't be bothered.

–That's good. I'm glad.

She relaxed her shoulders and staked both armrests.

—What will you do for money?

—I still have my grant money. I'm working at the university library.

The lights dimmed and their faces lit up blue.

9

Mary raised her hand. The director pointed to her.

—I'm a former sex worker. I was wondering why you didn't bother to tell the side of the prostitutes? They were just props for your narrative, faceless and nameless women you fucked and forgot about. Your movie is an insult to sex workers like me. How do you explain yourself?

Several people turned around. Pat sank in his seat and fanned his fingers over his face. *She must've rehearsed that speech*, Pat thought.

The director thrust his hands in the pockets of his corduroy jacket, pushed out his bottom lip, and furrowed his brow in a way that suggested her complaint was fair, but hard to judge.

—I understand your point of view. But I'm not a prostitute, I was the man addicted to them, and so it follows that I can't tell that story, the story of the prostitutes.

MEMORIES OF MY FRIEND ALEX, WHO IS DEAD.

1

My friend Alex is dead. He was 34 when he died.

2

At my seventh grade talent show, there was a tap-dancer, a magician, and a girl who hula-hooped. Then Alex and his two friends appeared on stage with two guitars and a drum kit.

Alex wore a ratty white t-shirt under a fuzzy baby blue cardigan, ripped jeans and Converse One

Stars. The other two guys in the band were dressed similarly.

They launched into a cover of "Smells Like Teen Spirit," a brand new song at the time. The crunch from the guitar and rhythm of the drum filled the entire gym. The Black and Latino boys began moshing.

Alex's band lost the talent show to a young girl who sang Whitney Houston's "Greatest Love of All" to the wonderment and joy of everyone who hadn't been kicked out for moshing.

3

Alex's parents were antique dealers. His house looked like a normal house on the outside, but inside it was the Library of Alexandria. There were piles of aged and obscure books. There were neoclassical tables and desks made of wood that seemed to glow. On the walls were 19th century landscape paintings in thick, gilded frames.

4

I'd heard Alex had jumped off someone's roof and hurt himself. Shortly after he was released from the hospital, he invited me over to his house to listen to a new record. I went because I wanted to check up on him, but I was also curious why anyone would buy records when CDs were readily available. I stepped back when he answered the door.

His face looked like someone had smashed it on the sidewalk then tried to glue it back on his head with red paint. Thick red cuts zigzagged his cheeks and forehead. The whites of his blue eyes were wine red. His lips were half-gone and swollen. The skin on his nose was gone. Half his teeth were gone.

He didn't try to hide it. He seemed to love how gross he looked. He held his head high and told me to come in.

"I smoked some crack and drank a lot of vodka, then I jumped off a roof and landed in someone's shed," he said, before laughing like someone laughing with a mask on.

The record he'd bought was *the "Priest" they called him,* which featured William S. Burroughs reading a story aloud while Kurt Cobain played guitar. The story was about a priest who gives the last bit of heroin to a young Mexican boy experiencing a harsh withdrawal on Christmas Eve.

I didn't understand why anyone would find this interesting, but Alex's broken face seemed to twitch at every sentence.

5

Six months later, his face was healed. There were no scars. Implants replaced his teeth and he looked more handsome than ever. He talked a lot about going to college. He dated the one cheerleader who always seemed depressed. I remember him telling me how this cheerleader was not like the others, that she was smart and understood people. They weren't together long, but they remained close friends after the relationship ended.

6

Alex was the first person I ever saw shoot up heroin. He sat on his red baroque couch, his right arm upturned, tied with a tourniquet and fixed between his knees. I remember the tiny depression forming on his vein before the needle broke into his skin. A little blood spurted into the syringe before he pushed its contents into his body. A little bit later, he asked if I wanted to try it. I said no. Sometimes I wonder what my life would be if I'd said yes.

7

Throughout high school, Alex lent me books. *On the Road, Howl, Junky, Lunch Poems.* As a black teenager with two white parents, they were books that made me feel okay with not fitting into the world. They taught me that art and drugs are the only respectable balms for the loneliness the world imposes on you.

8

I ran into Alex at a record store. I asked if he knew where I could get some weed and he said yes. We got into his old yellow diesel Mercedes. There were lots of cough syrup bottles in the backseat. He said the cough syrup contains dextromethorphan (DXM) and that he was experimenting with the drug. I remember thinking "I'm not gonna ask," before he launched into a speech about the history and effects of DXM.

9

Once Alex took me to his father's antiques warehouse in downtown Oklahoma City. Inside, the space was filled with relics: lamps, tables, paintings, books, globes, radios, couches. In the middle of all this stuff was a jet-black car with a cloud-white interior. Alex calmly explained that the car was a 1970-something Maserati.

"See the dashboard?" he said, pointing to the white dashboard, "It's made from a special type of white cork tree found only in southern Italy."

He ran his fingers along the hood in a way that seemed sensual.

"It doesn't run. But one day my dad and I are going to restore it."

I pictured Alex driving the Maserati on the highway, backseat full of cough syrup.

10

A couple days after 9/11, Alex and I took MDMA together at a party at the depressed cheerleader's house. About an hour into the party, Alex said he was feeling tired and wanted to go home. He said he couldn't drive me back to my dorm but that I could crash at his place. The depressed cheerleader begged Alex not to leave.

"The effects of MDMA are disappointing and unreal," he said, before opening the door.

The depressed cheerleader looked at me. I shrugged, confused by Alex's actions but also by the sensation of confusion.

At his house, he made a palette for me on the floor and set his AC window unit on full blast. He turned on CNN and muted the sound.

He fell asleep on his red baroque couch immediately. I was flat on the hard floor, freezing, jaw chattering, unable to move or sleep, watching the towers fall in silence, for hours.

11

Alex eventually left Oklahoma. He met a woman named Melissa on an online message board for heroin addicts. They fell in love and she convinced Alex to move to New York.

Melissa was an artist. She graduated from Cooper Union. She'd shown her work in galleries around the world. Her work was in the permanent collection at MoMA.

Like Alex, she loved heroin, and also like Alex, she loved heroin culture. She ran a popular blog that reviewed heroin products, warning other heroin users what was safe and what was not. She became famous within the opioid enthusiasts community and was later interviewed by a national publication under a pseudonym.

Like Alex, Melissa is dead.

12

Alex and Melissa left New York City and bounced around the country, using and selling heroin, before finally settling in Oklahoma. Alex inherited his uncle's modest house in a working class Oklahoma City suburb. Two years later, the house burned down and their bodies were found inside. Alex's throat was slit and Melissa suffered blunt force trauma to the head. Their bodies were in the house for a week before someone set fire to the place. That's all I know about what happened to my friend Alex, who is dead.

OPEN SPACES

LAUREN SCANNED THE PARKING GARAGE FOR her Honda Civic and saw it was further away than she thought. *I should've parked closer*, she said to herself, striding alongside the line of cars in big stretches. Once in her car, she texted Herman *I'm leaving, are you staying late tonight?* and dropped her iPhone in the cupholder.

She thought about going to Wendy's after she remembered reading on the internet that Wendy's chicken sandwiches are "antibiotic free." *That's important to me*, she thought. Herman would get mad if he knew she ate any kind of meat, especially from a chain like Wendy's.

She looked at herself in the rearview mirror and tried to judge the prominence of her second chin. After staring for several seconds she said *Ugh, fuck it* to herself in a low, gravelly voice, then glanced at her iPhone in the cupholder.

She drove to Wendy's.

"I'll have the chicken sandwich, the new one, with the bacon. And just the sandwich. And an un-sweet tea."

"Okay that will be $4.86."

"Did you get that? Un-sweet tea."

"Yes, ma'am we got it."

"Okay."

Lauren rolled up the window.

I have to check because last time you gave me the sweet tea and I don't want the sweet tea, I want the unsweet tea, she thought, *the sweet tea is like 12 tablespoons of sugar and 200 liquid calories, are you crazy, don't give me the sweet tea.*

Lauren pulled behind a Kia Sorrento and pictured black-suited MBAs in a room telling the Wendy's CEO that quality meat is the future of fast food. *"Antibiotic-free" but it's still mass killing*, she thought. She opened her iPhone and googled "Where does Wendy's get their chicken?" She read Wendy's gets chickens from a farm in New Zealand where they roam free, not in cages. She imagines telling Herman, "Look the chickens run free" and Herman replying, "They can say whatever they want on a website. Ultimately, an animal has to die."

I can't win with you, she thought, before imagining what it would be like to kick Herman in the leg. She often imagined kicking him in the leg when he began a monologue about her Republican dad, or her liking eating meat. She pictured him falling to the ground with a little scream. *I'm such a bitch*, she thought, smiling while opening Instagram. *I should Instagram my Wendy's*, she thought.

Her iPhone buzzed. She read a text from Herman: Yeah, I'll be late. Eat dinner without me. Love you.

The man at the window waved his arms to get her attention. Lauren rolled down the window of her Civic.

"Ma'am, $4.86. Would you like any condiments."

"No."

GLASSES

MY PARENTS HAD GLASSES. I WANTED GLASSES too.

My parents weren't talking to each other much, and they certainly weren't talking to me.

That could change if I had glasses.

If we all had glasses maybe we could get together and talk.

We'd talk about our eyesight, our lenses, our frames. We'd talk about how we always lose our glasses.

Mom would come home from work, take off her glasses, and place them on the coffee table. She'd do different things around the house, then stop and rub the bridge of her nose for a long time. She'd ask, "Where are my glasses?"

Dad's pair was thick and black-rimmed. He wore them with a strap around the earpieces. He wore them when he shaved.

My eyesight was perfect. 20/20. I passed every eye exam at school.

To get glasses, I had to fail the next eye exam.

"Go ahead and read the first line for me," the nurse said.

I saw W E R X S W A and read out "I Y E S Q A C."

"Hmmm," said the nurse, "try the next line."

I saw E H L Z O Q T and read out "M M V O J A O."

The nurse wrote something on a little slip of paper and handed it to me.

"Give this to your parents," the nurse said. The writing was a mess and I couldn't read it.

Dad was organizing his football cards in his office when I handed him the piece of paper. He looked at it and said, "Okay," in a way that conveyed "Okay, information received. Leave now." I looked at the boxes of football cards. I wanted Dad to talk to me about them, but disturbing him usually got me into trouble. I left and read comic books on the couch.

Mom arrived home and sat on the couch. She took her glasses off and rubbed the bridge of her nose. Dad showed Mom the nurse's note. Mom looked at the note and looked at me. Mom is a beautiful woman and it feels good when she looks at you. She turned to look for Dad, who had returned to the office with his football cards.

"You know you're going to have to take him?" Mom yelled through the wall.

She walked into Dad's office and closed the door. I could hear them yelling.

I looked at Mom's glasses on the coffee table. The frames were gold and the lenses thin. I reached for them and heard the office door open.

Mom walked out and said, "Where are my glasses?"

Dad was quiet as he drove. I was afraid of the eye doctor. I wanted him to let me know how it would go, but asking questions usually got me into trouble.

The eye doctor sat me down and asked me to look at the letters on the wall.

Where I saw W E R X S W A and I read out "I Y E S Q A C."

"Hmmm," he said, "Well, let's trying the next line."

I saw E H L Z O Q T and read out "M M V O J A O."

"Okay, hmm," he said.

The eye doctor reached into a desk and pulled out a pair of glasses. They were black-rimmed, like Dad's. I wanted them to be mine.

"Now let's try it with these," he said, handing me the glasses.

I put them on and looked at the wall with the letters.

I read out "W E R X S W A."

"Wonderful, thank you son," the eye doctor said.

I took off the glasses and handed them back to the doctor. The doctor folded them, put them in the desk, and left the room. Soon after, my father came in and motioned for me to follow him, which I did, out of the office and back to the car.

Dad was quiet in the car.

I wanted to know when I would get my glasses.

"When will I get my glasses?"

Dad smirked. "The glasses he gave you were fake."

I slumped my shoulders and put my forehead against the window.

It was a clear day.

I saw trees, people, and billboards zip by in a blur.

TIDE POOLS

"WE CAN GET TO THE TIDE POOLS BY THE beach trail out back. Or we can walk down highway one. The highway will be faster," Callie said.

Will stared at his phone and said *okay*. He was distracted by a tweet which posited Black people had, on average, lower IQs than white people.

He began to type a reply—*you piece of shit*—but he'd been obsessing over the tweet for an hour, and suddenly felt a sort of mental fatigue.

He put his phone to sleep and grabbed his puffer jacket. He put one arm in the puffer jacket, got a whiff of body odor, then stopped to sniff the sleeve.

"Eh, haven't washed this thing in a while actually. Sorry if I smell like B.O."

"Gross. Please wash it when we get home," Callie said, pulling at the puffer and examining it for stains.

"Okay," Will said in an annoyed tone, while imagining a young, obese white man with a thin goatee, wearing stained sweats, reeking of body odor and dandruff, sitting at a cluttered desk, clacking out on a giant black gaming keyboard: *it's scientific fact that blacks have lower IQs and liberals won't even let you talk about that.*

It's a scientific fact that you're a piece of human shit, Will thought, before imagining his account being suspended. He remembered seeing on CNN the police protecting a small band of white supremacists marching down the street in *What city was it* Will thought. *Shit, any city in America really.*

They set off down the small side road that led to the highway. Will realized they were about to walk on the shoulder of a busy highway, and that Callie had asked him about the best route. He said, "Wait, the beach trail is much prettier."

Much safer too, he thought.

Just a week ago, he was in his bedroom, fresh from the shower, when he heard a loud thump outside. Out the window, he saw a car speed off and an old Black man writhing in the street, his head covered in blood. The man's foot was nearly severed and dangled from his leg. He saw a skinny white teen in cargo shorts whisper-yelling, "oh shit oh shit oh shit" until a woman across the street shouted, "I called 9-1-1." The teen said, "okay okay okay!" while he waved his arms over the man in the street. The man was at least 60. *Hard to tell a Black man's age*, Will thought, picturing his Auntie Lisa saying "Black don't crack!" before throwing back a Heineken. He felt ashamed for smiling at this memory and having the urge to laugh while this man writhed and moaned just outside his bedroom window. He stood at the window in his underwear and watched the man struggle until the paramedics came and stretchered him away. Will got dressed and listened to two fire-women wash the blood from the street while discussing an episode of *The Bachelor.*

"C'mon. Let's take the beach trail. Look at the succulents. It's prettier," Will said, pointing at the beach trail.

"You already agreed. This is faster anyway. It's like a 100 feet," Callie said, gesturing to the highway shoulder as a string of cars whooshed by.

Will's ankles tingled. He pictured himself writhing on the lane marker, covered in blood, his foot nearly severed. He wanted to communicate this to Callie, but he couldn't think of a way to make his anxiety real for her. *Even if I could*, he thought, *she'd tell me to get over it so we can get to the tide pools faster*. By now they were nearly to the shoulder, and he could see how narrow the pathway was.

"Can we walk single file please?" Will said.

"Yeah, sure," she said, walking in front of him.

As they walked down the shoulder, Will focused on her heels, wincing as a PT cruiser passed. *Economic disenfranchisement negatively impacts IQ scores...*, Will thought, the lane marker in the corner of his eye, *There are no genetic determinants for one race being intellectually superior to another. Only someone who feels inferior would come to believe this is true.* He looked up and saw a Subaru with a "Feel the Bern" sticker moving away from him.

Oh we're here, Will thought. They were already on the neighborhood road leading up to the tide pools.

He noticed some houses in the neighborhood were neat modern box-houses and others were colonial shacks. He imagined someone in an upper bedroom, looking at him through a window, hoping he'd get hit by a car. Soon parked minivans populated the street and he could see the gates to the tide pools.

"Ugh, it's packed," said Callie.

Damn it's bright and people are everywhere, Will thought, his eyes squinting at the long slab of pockmarked rock that extended into the ocean. They walked through the parking lot to an asphalt path leading to the rock. Will looked at an energetic mother in hiking shoes alongside a glum-seeming dad in an earth-toned vest with two kids gripping sippy cups and running circles around them.

Will pictured himself asking: *Do you teach your children about white supremacy?* He imagined the mom saying to her child, "Whatever you learn in your history books, understand that Black people built America," and that child asking for a cookie.

Callie took Will's hand and she led him onto the rock.

"What's going on in that head of yours," she said, smiling back at him.

He wanted to tell her he was admiring the purple fog unrolling on the teal horizon, but he hadn't noticed it until now. He wanted to tell her he felt swallowed by the enormous sea, and the feeling made him accept his place in the universe, but he'd been ignoring the ocean. He wanted to tell her that being here with her, before the waves and the fog, felt romantic in a way that wasn't embarrassing, on account of her warm hand in his, but he'd been ignoring this feeling. All he could think about was this racist stranger on Twitter.

"Nothing. Just taking it all in," he replied.

Will looked down and saw small pools of glistening seawater. Some of the pools had crabs or small anemone inside. *They are vacationing in these craters*, Will thought, *until the tide comes back in and pushes them back out to sea, to find food, to find a mate, to die.* He sensed an urge to curl up and submerge himself in one of these tiny pools. *Wish I could stay in this tide pool forever*, Will thought. He heard Callie mention the streaks of red on the slicked back of a nearby crab.

Timothy Willis Sanders is the author of *Orange Juice and Other Stories* (Publishing Genius 2010) and the novel *Matt Meets Vik* (CCM 2014).
He lives in San Francisco.